PRODIGIES UNLEASHED

Crown Jewels Vol III

M S DHONI GLOBAL SCHOOL

notionpress.com

INDIA · SINGAPORE · MALAYSIA

ISBN
Hardcase 979-8-89632-761-5
Paperback 979-8-89632-310-5

CONTENTS

FOREWORD BY MR. MS DHONI

It brings me great pride and joy to introduce *Prodigies Unleashed – Crown Jewels Vol II & Vol III,* a testament to the immense talent and creativity cultivated at M S Dhoni Global School. In our journey to provide a holistic and forward-thinking education, this anthology stands as a milestone, showcasing the voices of our young authors from the Hosur and Bangalore campuses.

Just as cricket requires both individual dedication and teamwork, storytelling too involves a blend of personal insight and the guidance of mentors. Through these stories, I see the students' unique perspectives come to life, reflecting their courage, imagination, and curiosity about the world. Their work inspires not only the readers but also a generation of students who, through such platforms, realize that their ideas are valuable and impactful.

This compilation of stories celebrates the determination of each student to express themselves and take pride in their creativity. As they embrace storytelling, they take steps toward becoming confident communicators and thoughtful leaders—qualities that will serve them well in all their future pursuits. This book, in essence, is a celebration of their journey, one that I am honoured to support.

My heartiest congratulations to the students and faculty of M S Dhoni Global School. As you turn these pages, may you be inspired by the creativity and courage displayed here, knowing that this is just the beginning for these talented authors.

Yours,

MS Dhoni

FOREWORD BY DR. KANNAN GIREESH

It gives me immense pleasure to write the foreword for Prodigies Unleashed – Crown Jewels Vol II & Vol III, a compilation that not only celebrates the creativity and imagination of the students at M S Dhoni Global School but also aligns with the values we hold dear through the Leader in Me program.

As a firm believer in the power of education to shape the leaders of tomorrow, I see this anthology as a testament to the incredible potential of our young minds. The stories shared in these pages reflect the diversity of thought, vision, and expression that define the students of the Hosur and Bangalore campuses. They have woven tales from different genres—adventure, mystery, fantasy, and drama—giving us a glimpse into their boundless creativity and an insight into how they view the world around them.

At Live Life Education, we are committed to nurturing leaders who are not only academically competent but also emotionally intelligent, socially responsible, and compassionate. This anthology, while showcasing the imaginative works of our students, also serves as an inspiration to them. It teaches them that leadership begins with self-expression, the courage to share one's ideas, and the ability to grow through every experience.

What stands out in this collection is the authenticity and honesty with which these young authors have shared their stories. These works are a reminder that creativity is a muscle that must be exercised, and through such platforms, we are equipping our students with the tools they need to become confident communicators and thoughtful leaders.

I am proud of the students for embracing this opportunity to express themselves and for the mentors who have guided them in their journey. Congratulations to the students of M S Dhoni Global School for their outstanding work. I look forward to witnessing your continued growth and success as writers, thinkers, and leaders of tomorrow.

Sincerely,

Dr. Kannan Gireesh
Founder, Live Life Education

FOREWORD BY MR. BHAVIN SHAH

It is a true privilege to contribute the foreword to Prodigies Unleashed – Crown Jewels Vol II & Vol III, a reflection of the boundless creativity fostered at M S Dhoni Global School. This school has long championed an educational vision that combines rigorous academics with platforms for personal growth, cultivating an environment where students are inspired to pursue their creative and intellectual passions.

This anthology exemplifies that vision, bringing together stories across genres—from mystery and adventure to heartfelt drama. It highlights the unique voices of students from the Hosur and Bangalore campuses and celebrates their journey as budding authors, offering readers a genuine glimpse into their imaginations.

Through works like this, M S Dhoni Global School empowers students to explore new ideas, communicate effectively, and understand the transformative power of storytelling. It's my hope that this book will not only inspire its readers but also remind these young authors of the importance of curiosity, resilience, and self-expression on their journey to becoming the next generation of thinkers and leaders.

Congratulations to the students and mentors who have dedicated themselves to this project. May Prodigies Unleashed be the first step of many as you continue your journey of growth and achievement.

Regards,

Mr. Bhavin Shah
CEO & Director, Education World

PREFACE

Prodigies Unleashed – Crown Jewels Vol II & Vol III is a celebration of creativity, imagination, and the potential of the young minds at M S Dhoni Global School. This collection, featuring the voices of students from both the Hosur (Vol II) and Bangalore (Vol III) campuses, brings together a range of stories that explore various genres—from adventure and mystery to fantasy and heartfelt drama.

Each story in this anthology represents a unique perspective, a glimpse into the thoughts and dreams of students who are beginning their journey as writers. This compilation is not about perfection; it is about growth, learning, and discovery. By giving our students a platform to express themselves, we hope to encourage them to explore their creativity, understand the power of storytelling, and develop their voices as authors.

Through this book, we aim to foster the values of leadership, resilience, and self-expression, helping our students realize that their creativity is a valuable asset in becoming leaders not only in their chosen fields but also in their communities. This anthology serves as a stepping stone, motivating our young writers to continue developing their skills and confidence, paving the way for a future where their stories will continue to inspire and lead.

We are proud of our students for taking the first steps in their literary journey. This anthology is a reflection of their hard work, imagination, and determination. May it serve as a reminder that the path to greatness begins with a single word, a single story, and a single dream.

ACKNOWLEDGMENT

Ideas transform into reality through collective effort, inspiration, and unwavering support. As we unveil *Prodigies Unleashed – Crown Jewels Vol II*, we take a moment to reflect on the journey that brought this book to life and express our heartfelt gratitude to those who made it possible.

At the forefront of this endeavour is our school mentor, Mr. Mahendra Singh Dhoni, an inspiration to millions of youth in India and around the world. His remarkable career and commitment to excellence are a testament to the values we instill at M S Dhoni Global School. Our students have had the unparalleled privilege of engaging closely with him as a mentor. His campus visit, where he interacted personally with every student, left a lasting impact, motivating them to dream big and persevere. His foreword for this anthology beautifully reflects his encouragement for students to embrace creativity as a stepping stone toward leadership and self-expression.

We are equally honoured to have the continued association of Dr. Kannan Gireesh and Mr. Bhavin Shah, close acquaintances of our school for many years. Our sincere thanks also extend to Dr. Kannan Gireesh, a renowned psychiatrist, psychotherapist, and founder of Live Life

Education. His foreword highlights the role of creativity in leadership and personal development. Dr. Gireesh's commitment to holistic education aligns perfectly with the values we aim to instill in our students.

We are privileged to feature the insights of Mr. Bhavin Shah, CEO, and Director of EducationWorld, whose foreword celebrates the transformative power of storytelling. A pioneer in educational thought leadership, his encouragement motivates us to create platforms where students can express themselves fearlessly and explore their intellectual horizons.

This journey would not have been possible without the invaluable support of the school management. Our deepest gratitude goes to Mr. Chandrasekar, Chairman; Mrs. Bhuvaneswari Chandrasekar, Chairperson; Mr. Vineeth Chandrasekar, Vice-Chairman & Director (Admin & Operations); Mrs. Deepitha, Director (HR); Mr. Vishnu Gaurav Selvaraj, Director (IT & Sports); and Mrs. Nikitha, Director (Admissions & Onboarding). Their vision and encouragement were instrumental in creating this platform for students to showcase their creativity.

We extend heartfelt thanks to the school principal, Mrs. Lakshmi Prakash, for her relentless support and belief in the potential of this project. The commitment of the coordinators, Mrs. Saritha Changal and Mrs. Swati Pramod Amodkar, the teachers, and the Design and Technical team ensured this book reached the highest standards of quality and creativity.

A special acknowledgment is extended to the exceptional members of our English Team who were directly involved in the meticulous process of compiling and refining this anthology. Their relentless dedication and collaborative effort have been pivotal in transforming this vision into reality. We sincerely appreciate the hard work of Mrs. Vanitha .K, Mrs. Ankita Sengupta, Mrs. Gomatheeswari Bhaskaran, Mrs. Amitha V.V, Mrs. Priya Vardeene, Ms. Devika T S, Mrs. Gouri Hegde, Mrs. Vani M, Mrs. Rupali Rawal, Mrs. Vipanchee Gogoi, Mrs. Debarpita G Upadhyay, and myself, Mrs. Farzana A, for their significant contributions.

Finally, we extend our heartfelt congratulations to the young authors whose creativity and hard work have brought this book to life. Each story is a testament to their imagination and dedication. As a team, we are proud to celebrate their journey and look forward to seeing their talents flourish in the years to come.

01

WHEN THE SKY REMEMBERS

– AARIN SINGH

The sky was bright and empty over Raju's village in Rajasthan. It hadn't rained for so long that the ground was cracked and dry. The plants in Amma's small field were drooping, their leaves turning brown. Each day, water became harder to find, and Raju worried more and more.

One evening, as Amma poured the last bit of water into Raju's cup, he looked up and asked, "Amma, why won't the rain come? Has it forgotten us?"

Amma said softly, "No, beta. Sometimes, we have to wait and trust. My mother told me that when the skies are quiet, we just need to hold on. The rain will come when it's ready."

Raju tried to believe her words. Every morning, he carried their little bit of water to the plants, gently pouring drops on their roots and whispering, "Just hold on." At night, he and Amma would sit outside, looking up at the stars, hoping the sky would remember them.

Then, one hot morning, as Raju lifted the empty bucket, he felt something cool on his cheek. He touched his face and looked up. Another drop fell—and then another. Dark clouds filled the sky, rumbling softly, and soon rain was pouring down.

The rain soaked the ground, filling the air with the smell of fresh, wet earth. Amma's eyes filled with happy tears. She laughed, and together they ran outside, holding hands, dancing as the rain fell. They splashed in the soft mud, and Raju felt the cool raindrops washing away the dust.

Amma hugged him tightly and said, "Do you see, beta? The rain always remembers. We just needed to believe and wait."

Many years later, Raju would tell his own children about that day and teach them, just as Amma had taught him, to be patient and hopeful. For, sometimes, we must wait for the sky to remember.

Moral: Good things take time, and if we wait patiently, they will come when we need them most.

Author's Profile:

Aarin is an observant and reflective student with a unique ability to find the extraordinary in the ordinary. His thoughtful narratives showcase a deep curiosity and empathy, allowing him to connect with the emotions of others and highlight the beauty of shared human experiences. Through his creative thinking and articulate expression, Aarin transforms familiar moments into meaningful stories that inspire and resonate with readers.

02

THE MYSTERIOUS ISLAND

– NAINIKA KANIKE

There was a loud noise on the pirate ship, and everyone was in a state of hustle and bustle, wondering what had gone wrong. They decided to steer the ship to a nearby island. As they disembarked, they saw rows of houses and were surprised to find that no one was living there.

A little later, a boy with tiny toes and a pale appearance slowly emerged from one of the houses. The pirates wondered how he had survived there all alone. After speaking with him, they learned that his name was Sam, and he was only seven years old. He had not eaten enough for many days. The pirates shared the food they had left with Sam.

The pirates couldn't understand how he had been left alone on the island, as the boy spoke in a language they did not understand. However, they were glad to have found him. The pirates searched the island thoroughly but found no one else besides Sam.

After some time, a tsunami began to approach the island. The pirates panicked, unsure of what to do. Sam pointed at something, and when they went to investigate, they discovered a secret passage. Everyone hurried inside the passage to hide as the tsunami flooded the island.

The pirates praised the boy and thanked him for saving their lives. Using gestures, they invited him to join them, and Sam happily accepted, setting off with the pirates on their next adventure.

Author's Profile:

Nainika is a curious and imaginative child who sees the world as full of puzzles waiting to be solved. She often observes details others might miss and have a knack for asking questions that lead to surprising answers. She enjoys weaving suspense into stories, keeping everyone on the edge of their seat. Her mind is constantly analysing situations, finding the unexpected in the ordinary. She exhibits deep love for solving mysteries and a strong sense of justice.

03

THE HAVELI'S SECRET SMILE

– KYRA BAGGA

At the edge of the village, near the quiet banks of the Yamuna River, stood an old Haveli, forgotten and overgrown with plants. The elders whispered that it had been empty for generations. Some said the spirit of a young girl named Anjali still lingered there, waiting for someone to play with her.

One evening, Rohan, a curious 10-year-old, along with his friends Priya and Amit, dared each other to step inside. With lanterns in hand, they pushed open the heavy wooden door, which creaked like an old tabla being struck. The musty air was thick with the scent of sandalwood and dust, making their hearts race.

"Let's not stay too long," Priya said, gripping Rohan's arm tightly.

They tiptoed across marble floors covered in cracked tiles, with shadows dancing in the dim light. Just as they were about to retreat, a soft tinkling sound echoed from the grand staircase. Amit's eyes widened. "Did you hear that?" he whispered, barely breathing.

Rohan swallowed hard. "We should see what it is," he said, sounding braver than he felt. They climbed the ornate steps, decorated with faded peacock engravings, each creak echoing like a beat from a dhol.

At the top, they discovered a room draped in faded silks. A cracked mirror stood in the corner, and a small clay doll with one missing arm lay on a cushioned stool. Suddenly, the mirror glowed, and an image of a girl in a traditional lehenga appeared. Her face was gentle, and her eyes glimmered with longing.

"Don't be afraid," the girl whispered. "I am Anjali. I have waited for friends."

The children exchanged glances, their initial fear melting away. Anjali's smile was warm and inviting. They realized she wasn't there to haunt them, but to join in the laughter and games she missed so dearly. That night, the Haveli echoed not with ghostly wails, but with the cheerful giggles of children and the soft notes of a ghostly harmonium.

From that day on, the old Haveli became a place not of fear, but of stories where friends from two worlds met to share joy and friendship.

Author's Profile:

Kyra is a creative child with a flair for the eerie and supernatural. They have a vivid imagination, often conjuring up spine-chilling tales that leave everyone with goosebumps.

Her thought process is thrillingly unpredictable, expertly building suspense and keeping the reader hooked until the end. She is deeply interested in exploring emotions like fear and mystery, using words to evoke powerful feelings.

04

THE MYSTERY OF SPACE

– ABHAY H Y

One day a boy named John visited his grandparents' house, and there he found a book. He took the book and opened it, and the book's ink started to change colour from blue to black and from black to green, etc. His grandfather wrote about his journey in space. His grandfather's journey started on "June 12, 1981". John's grandfather found a planet that had sharp teeth, large eyes, webbed feet and fins instead of fins.

The monster saw the grandfather and started to run towards him. He ran into his rocket and launched onto another planet it had trees which had leaves of blue colour, green coloured lake, and had red sun. There were aliens instead of humans, they had shops and houses.

They were selling bread and cookies that had cockroaches and blood in them which was very disgusting.

The aliens saw the grandfather and started to shoot with a laser gun. He launched his rocket to Earth and landed safely. John went and asked his grandfather about his journey. His grandfather said that the planets do not exist.

He went through a portal of planets which was in outer space.

Hence, it was a mystery.

Author's Profile:

Abhay is a highly imaginative and creative student who excels in storytelling. His ability to explore complex ideas, such as parallel worlds, reflects his intellectual curiosity and originality. Through his narratives, he captivates readers with compelling adventures and meaningful themes of self-discovery. Abhay's innovative mindset and articulate communication skills allow him to express his thoughts with clarity and depth, making his stories both engaging and thought-provoking.

05

THE DETECTIVE

– KARUNYA K GOWDA

In the small town of Mysore, everyone knew each other. One sunny morning, Sita found out that her necklace was missing. She was very upset and called the Detective to help find it. The detective came quickly and started asking questions. He first talked to Sita. "When did you last see your necklace?" he asked.

"I wore it to the fair yesterday," Sita said. "I remember taking it off before bed. "The detective then talked to the housekeeper. "Did you see the necklace?" he asked.

The housekeeper shook her head. "No, sir. I cleaned the house this morning, but I didn't see it."

Next, the detective talked to Sita's neighbor. "Did you notice anything unusual?" he asked.

The neighbor thought for a moment. "I saw a man in a red jacket near Sita's house last night," he said. The detective thanked the neighbour and kept investigating.

He searched the house carefully and found a small piece of red cloth near the window. He also saw that the window was a little open.

With this clue, the Detective went to the local tailor. "Have you seen anyone with a torn red jacket?" he asked.

The tailor nodded. "Yes, Mr. Sham came in this morning to fix his jacket. "Detective quickly went to Mr. Sham's house. After a short talk, Sham confessed. "I needed money and thought the necklace would help," he said.

The detective returned the necklace to Sita, who was very thankful. The mystery was solved.

Author's Profile:

Karunya's storytelling quality reflects her sharp intellect, creativity, and keen attention to detail. Her ability to craft complex plots demonstrates her analytical thinking and imaginative problem-solving skills. She has a natural flair for engaging her audience, weaving suspenseful narratives that keep readers on the edge of their seats. Her determination to create compelling stories highlights her focus and perseverance, while her passion for storytelling shines through in her dedication to delivering captivating and thought-provoking tales.

06

THE MAGICAL SNAKE

– NABHAY V

CHAPTER 1

Long ago, there was an island far away from India. It was a huge island of dense forest with exotic animals and birds. The people of India have named this island the *"Magical Island"*.

This island was ruled by a King named *"Shine"* who was a beautiful and sparkling Snake. The Indians called him *"The Magical Snake"*, because of the magical powers he had. At the same time, he was a kind and truthful king. He loved all the animals in the forest. They all praised him for his welfare. The Zebra, Ostrich, and the Peacock were his closest friends and helped him deal with the problems of the animals. He was a powerful ruler.

CHAPTER 2

The kindness and magical strengths of King Shine made the hunters in India very jealous. The hunters wanted to kill him break his magical horn on the forehead and sell it to the King of Pondicherry, which would fetch them a lot of money.

But the hunters thought that it wasn't easy to kill and capture the Magical Snake. They decided to find a creature as huge as the Magical Snake which could fight with him. So, they left for the Magical Island using their boats and crossed the Indian Ocean. As they reached the island, they saw a huge creature with huge claws and sharp teeth. They thought that it wasn't easy to summon it as it was a huge Dragon.

Then the hunters started thinking of ways to convince it. Then one of them suggested that *'we could make a magical portion using the magical ingredients in the forest so that we can make the Dragon believe that we are his Commanders"*. They collected the ingredients, made a magical portion, and gave it to the Dragon. The Dragon obliged to the hunters immediately after drinking it. The Dragon followed the instructions given by the hunters.

CHAPTER 3

The hunters along with the Dragon went to fight the mighty King Shine. The King was shocked to hear this as he did not want war. The hunters trickily locked the other animals in the forest. This made the Snake fight all alone with the hunters and the Dragon. Both the Magical Snake and the Dragon had a fierce fight.

The Snake used all his magical power to defend himself against the Dragon and at last he cast the magical spell *"Rainbow Blast"* and created a huge sparkling rainbow. This enormous rainbow destroyed the hunters and made the

Dragon a normal creature like any other animal. The Dragon was very thankful to the King.

After the fierce battle, the island came back to its normalcy. Everyone praised the King for his generosity towards the Dragon and admired his magical powers. The King and the other animals along with the Dragon lived happily ever after.

Author's Profile:

Nabhay is a dedicated and creative student known for his sincerity and positive attitude. He carries kindness and integrity in both his actions and words, making him a role model for his peers. Nabhay's natural leadership qualities shine through in group activities, where his calm demeanor and ability to listen inspire others.

07

THE KNOCK

– NITHYA SAHASRA

Sarah had just moved into an old, quiet house, hoping for peace after the chaos of city life. But every night, without fail, she heard a knock at the door—soft at first, then louder, deliberate. Tap... tap... tap... pause... then a final, sharp knock.

One night, unable to take it any longer, Sarah decided to wait by the door. At midnight, the knocks came again. Tap... tap... tap... pause... and the last knock, louder than ever.

She opened the door, her heart pounding.

No one was there.

But something caught her eye—scratched into the doorframe were the words: *"I'm not knocking anymore"*

The door slammed shut. And in the silence, Sarah realized the knocking hadn't come from outside. It had been from within.

Author's Profile:

Nitya is a creative and imaginative student with a remarkable talent for storytelling. Her ability to weave suspenseful and meaningful narratives reflects her deep understanding of human emotions and her knack for crafting engaging plots. With vivid descriptions and a relatable protagonist, Nitya captures the essence of wonder and bravery, drawing readers into her world of fantasy.

08

A NIGHT AT THE FAIR!

– ANKITA R

It was a bright night; people, cheerful and gaily dressed, strolled around the fair, enjoying the sound of the drums that were usually played during the festival. Bonny, a young girl, was no exception. She was beaming with excitement as she gazed at the colourful stalls and the vibrant lights. She had been looking forward to this day for weeks, and she was not going to let anything ruin her fun.

As she walked through the fair, she came across a stall selling handmade jewellery. The necklaces, earrings, and bracelets were intricately designed and adorned with precious stones. Bonny was fascinated. She decided to buy a necklace for her mother as a surprise gift. She looked around the stall and finally settled on a beautiful silver necklace with a sapphire pendant.

A SURPRISE GIFT (Scene 1)

She handed over the money, the vendor gave her a curious look. He said –" are you sure you want to buy this necklace? It is said that this brings bad luck to whoever wears it."

Bonny was taken aback when the vendor's warning, but she did not let it defer her. She had come this far and was not going to let a silly superstition ruin her plans. She smiled at the vendor and said, " I do not believe in superstitions. This necklace is beautiful, and my mother would love it."

The vendor shrugged and gave her the sapphire necklace in a special box covered in a heart wrapping paper with a note saying –" thank you for everything, Mom!" And" The best mom ever!"

Bonny thanked the vendor and hurried away, eager to give her mother the surprise gift. When Bonny presents the necklace, her mother is overjoyed. Her mother said –" It is the most beautiful necklace I have ever seen, thank you, my child."

MOTHER'S LOVE (Scene 1)

From that day onwards, whenever Bonny's mother would wear the necklace, she would be overjoyed. The necklace brought them both good luck instead of bad luck because it was a symbol of love and a special night at the fair!!!....

Author's Profile:

Ankita is a deeply imaginative and insightful student whose storytelling reflects a unique blend of creativity and emotional intelligence. Ankita's ability to balance originality with universal appeal demonstrates her versatility as a writer. Her dedication to crafting meaningful and engaging stories reflects her determination and passion for storytelling, making her a truly gifted and inspiring young writer.

09

FROZEN

– DHRUTI P

Once upon a time there lived two sisters named Elsa and Anna with their parents who were the king and queen. They were living happily. One day they were playing with the snow when Elsa accidentally froze Anna's heart by touching her with fingers. They went to the wizard to see Anna.

Elsa could not control her powers, so she was locked up in a room. After some days their parents went to the dark sea by ship. It was a stormy night, and the boat sank and they died. After years passed a day came when everyone gathered to announce Elsa as a queen.

They gave her a lamp to hold as she was the new queen of the kingdom, but the lamp turned into ice and her secret was revealed so she left the castle and ran away far from the kingdom. Anna tried to stop her, but she could not. The kingdom was frozen wherever she walked. Anna, Kristohf, Sven- the Reindeer who was her friend decided to bring back Elsa to the kingdom.

After travelling days far, they found her on a mountain, but she refused to come back, then Anna tried to convince her by saying the kingdom is covered with snow and you are the only one who could change by bringing everything back to normal. "So please come back my sister" she said. Finally, she was convinced, and they both came back to the kingdom. She used her powers to change the snow into water and it went to the sea. They lived happily ever after.

Author's Profile:

Dhruti is a highly imaginative and versatile student whose storytelling talent shines through in her ability to blend fantasy with mystery seamlessly. Her unique perspective and creative thinking allow her to craft narratives that are both captivating and thought-provoking. Dhruti's skill in merging genres reflects her innovative approach to writing and her willingness to experiment with ideas. Her passion for storytelling, combined with her originality and depth, makes her an inspiring and exceptional writer.

10

THE WHISPERING SHADOWS OF LUNARIA

– MANEET TIRUVEEDI

In the forgotten town of Lunaria, cradled between steep, shadowy hills and a dense, whispering forest, an age-old secret brewed beneath the cobblestone streets and ivy-clad walls. The town, perpetually shrouded in twilight even at noon, held an air of timelessness that made it a haven for those seeking refuge from the bustling world beyond.

Elara, a young woman with raven-black hair and eyes mirrored the midnight sky, had lived in Lunaria all her life. Her grandmother often spoke of the "whispering shadows" that flitted through the streets at dusk, tales of ghostly figures that spoke in hushed tones, carrying messages from the past. Most dismissed these stories as the ramblings of an old woman, but Elara sensed a deeper truth within them.

One evening, as the town settled into its usual eerie quiet, Elara wandered into the forest. The trees, ancient and gnarled, seemed to watch her with knowing eyes. A cool breeze rustled the leaves, carrying the faint sound of whispers. Following the murmurs, she found herself at the edge of a secluded clearing where an old, abandoned mansion stood. Its once grand structure was now a decaying ruin, overrun with creeping vines and moss.

Elara felt an inexplicable pull towards the mansion. As she stepped through the creaking door, the whispers grew louder, swirling around her like a living thing. The air was thick with the scent of decay and the memories of a bygone era. Moonlight filtered through shattered windows, casting ghostly patterns on the dusty floor.

In the grand hall, Elara found an ornate mirror covered in a thick layer of grime. With a sense of urgency, she wiped away the dust to reveal her reflection. But instead of her face, she saw the visage of a young woman, strikingly like herself, yet clad in the fashion of centuries past. The woman's eyes were filled with a mix of sorrow and longing.

"Elara," the woman's voice echoed in her mind, "I am your ancestor, Eveline. The shadows whisper our family's curse, a curse bound by a broken promise and the restless spirits of Lunaria. You must lift the curse before it consumes us all."

Eveline's story unfolded in Elara's mind—a tale of love, betrayal, and a promise to protect Lunaria that had been shattered by greed. The spirits of those wronged, unable to move on, had become the whispering shadows, forever bound to the town.

Determined to set things right, Elara sought the wisdom of her grandmother's tales and the guidance of the whispers. She learned of a hidden chamber beneath the mansion, where a sacred relic, the Heart of Lunaria, lay dormant. It was said to have the power to heal the rift and free the spirits.

With newfound courage, Elara ventured into the chamber, guided by the whispers. She found the Heart of Lunaria, a pulsating crystal imbued with ancient magic. As she placed her hands upon it, a surge of energy coursed through her, and the shadows began to coalesce into radiant figures.

"Thank you," Eveline's voice whispered one last time. "You have restored our honor and given us peace."

As dawn broke over Lunaria, the shadows dissipated, leaving the town bathed in a gentle, golden light. The whispers had ceased, but their memory lived on in Elara's heart, a testament to the enduring power of love and redemption.

Author's Profile:

Maneet has developed a strong passion for writing, using his creative skills to articulate his ideas and thoughts. His curiosity for exploring new topics shines through in his work. Naturally gifted in communication, he confidently shares his perspectives, captivating his peers with his storytelling. With his growing talent for both writing and speaking, he effortlessly engages others, bringing his ideas to life with ease.

SPANDANA RV

MRIDHIMA AGARWAL

RIYANSHI MAHESWARI

AMONA CHAVADI

ANKITA R

I AM AN AUTHOR

ABHAY H Y

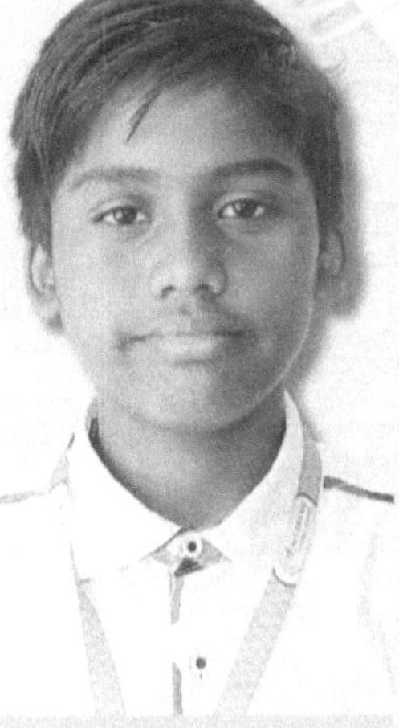

MANEET TIRUVEEDI

K SAHANA

ADITYA HEGDE

NITHYA SAHASRA

11

AN ENCHANTING FOREST

– AADRITI

Once upon a time, there lived a girl named Isabel. She was curious, enthusiastic, and interested in imaginary animals like unicorns. She was determined and dedicated to finding a real unicorn, as she believed that unicorns do exist hiding from humans.

One day Isabel set her journey to find a real unicorn, she went to some caves which were called "The Crystal Caves". As soon as she reached the cave she started exploring, there were lots of unique crystals in different colours, shapes, and sizes.

As she was walking through the cave, she saw something colourful and pointy and heard a galloping sound, Isabel followed the sound until she reached the end of the cave. Isabel was surprised, there was an enchanted world at the end of the cave.

Suddenly she saw the same colourful and pointy thing behind a tall tree, Isabel thought it was it, her dream had come true, as soon as she looked behind the tree, she was surprised to see a real unicorn. Isabel didn't want to go home, she wanted to stay there in the enchanted world with the majestic unicorn, and suddenly she heard an alarm.

It was a dream!' What a wonderful dream it has been, said Isabel to herself.

Author's Profile:

Aadriti is a talented storyteller who crafted a captivating tale about The Crystal Cave, a mystical place that challenges the inner strength of all who enter. Her vivid descriptions bring the setting to life, immersing readers in its enchanting yet formidable atmosphere. With a relatable protagonist, she skillfully explores courage, resilience, and self-discovery. Her ability to weave a gripping narrative keeps readers engaged, while her imaginative storytelling sparks curiosity and inspires reflection.

12

ALIENS AROUND US

– CHAKRAVARTHY SASSIKUMAR

Year 2100,

It started when the smartest people from Earth and Electro (man-made planet) were selected to go to the Moon for an important meeting in an area called Techno 59.00 Ar. There the president of the Moon announced that some selected smart people are going to 5 different planets in a system called the AR system.

They will be going in a huge spaceship called the Expanded Rocket Landers Station (ERLS). There will be 4 captains, 10 doctors and nurses, 10 army men, 6 very smart families and 15 humanoid robots. They started their journey in 2120. It took 55 years to reach the system. Now they have finally reached the AR system.

The first planet had very smart Aliens and because they were not parasites, the crew went onto the planet and became friends. They stayed on that planet and said goodbye and went to the other planet. The second planet also had Aliens but were very greedy and poorly advanced. And they hate anyone coming to their planet, so they invaded it. Then they went to the third planet which had a Mars-like surface. So, they kept the flag and went. The fourth planet was the same so they kept the flag and went. The fifth planet had parasites so the robots could only go there. Thankfully they didn't find any parasites, so they safely returned.

Now we have 2 Alien planets around us. They are friendly with us; this helps in expanding our home beyond the solar system and the Milky Way.

Author's Profile:

Chakravarthi is an incredible imagination, crafting stories about futuristic worlds and advanced technology. He has a curious mind and a talent for explaining complex concepts in an engaging way. Passionate about storytelling, they explore exciting themes like artificial intelligence and humanity's future. With his creativity and curiosity, they show great potential as a writer and thinker.

13

RICKY AND HIS MYSTERIOUS ADVENTURE

– CHIRAG VASANTH

Ricky, the brave, the smart, the adventurous, lived in an apartment in California. He loved to play and explore new things. During this time, his exams were ongoing. As days passed, his exams finally ended. He exclaimed, "Finally, my exams are over!" and walked into his flat. It was 7:00 p.m. He planned to do something very mischievous and sneaked out of the house. He ran towards the park and happily swung on the swings.

Suddenly, he saw a portal appear in front of him. It powerfully sucked everything in, including Ricky. Out of nowhere, he found himself at a mysterious temple, hidden in the deepest depths of the forest, a place that only the worthiest could find. As he bravely approached the temple's entrance, Ricky's stomach was in knots. He felt like he was losing heart when he realized something strange was happening in the garden. He grabbed a torch from the wall. At that moment, he gained courage for the first time in his life. He couldn't believe his eyes.

He saw a book marked with an "M." When he touched it, he started spinning so fast that he could barely see anything. After a few seconds, he found himself on an empty beach. It was very strange. He began exploring the beach and noticed strange letters on the rocks, hiding something. As he walked towards the water, he randomly teleported back near his apartment. He rushed inside, ran into his flat, and collapsed in his room, exhausted. Nobody knows where the portal came from. It had been a mysterious adventure for Ricky.

Author's Profile:

Chirag's storytelling reflects his inquisitive mind, boundless creativity, and a passion for discovery. His fascination with how things work fuels his ability to craft intricate, futuristic worlds grounded in realism and innovation. Chirag's imaginative thinking is complemented by a problem-solving mindset, allowing him to invent extraordinary concepts and weave them seamlessly into his narratives. His curiosity and sense of wonder drive him to explore uncharted ideas, making his stories both captivating and thought-provoking.

14

INTO MY CHOCOLATE WORLD!!

– SRIRANJINI K

Dusshhhhhhh!!! I woke up and saw that it was raining chocolate! The world around me was completely filled with sweets and chocolates. I was drenched in chocolate, and as I looked around, I realized I was alone. The ground beneath me was soft, like marshmallows. The trees were made of licoricey, their branches swaying gently in the breeze. The air smelled sweet, like a blend of vanilla, strawberry, and chocolate fudge. When I grabbed a piece of chocolate and tasted it, it was like nothing I had ever had before—it was the most delicious chocolate imaginable.

Suddenly, I heard a soft voice saying, "Welcome to the world of sweets!" At first, I was shocked because there seemed to be nobody around. Then, I noticed a small bird sitting on a nearby tree. I couldn't believe my eyes—a talking bird! I was scared at first, but the bird was so friendly that we quickly became close friends. We talked for a while, but one question kept nagging at me. "How did you come here?" I asked.

The bird gave me a simple answer: "I was born here." After some time, the bird said it was getting late and flew off, promising that we would meet again the next day. I continued walking until I heard a sound, *whoooshooooo!* It was a chocolate fountain! I couldn't control my excitement and love for chocolate. When I tried to take some, I slipped and fell in. I panicked because I didn't know how to swim and began to sink.

Just then, I saw a woman in the distance. She swam over, touched me, and said, "Wake up, wake up." Suddenly, I woke up to find that there was no chocolate rain or magical world. I was back in my bed at home. Oh! It had all been a dream!

Author's Profile:

Sriranjini is imaginative, joyful, and creative, with a talent for bringing magical worlds to life. She is empathetic and has an expressive storytelling style that captivates and inspires her audience. Her positive outlook and ability to create wonder-filled narratives reflect her warm and uplifting personality.

15

THE ADVENTURE OF MIRA AND THE LOST TEMPLE

– ISHANI SALIMATH

Once upon a time, there was a curious girl named Mira, who loved exploring and discovering new things. One day, she found an old book titled *The Mystery of the Lost Temple* on her bookshelf. Excited, she ran to her father, who was tending the garden, and asked him about it. Her father explained that the book told of an ancient Ganesha temple in Hampi that had mysteriously disappeared thousands of years ago and had never been found since. Intrigued, Mira wanted to go to Hampi to uncover the lost temple herself. Although Hampi was far from their home, her father suggested that she visit her grandparents, who lived nearby, and explore the site from there.

The next day, Mira traveled to her grandparents' home and met up with her friend. Together, they decided to embark on the adventure of a lifetime: finding the lost Ganesha temple. For days, they roamed through Hampi, exploring ancient ruins, learning about the culture, and soaking in the history of the place. One day, they encountered a wise old saint who, after hearing about their mission, hinted that the lost temple might still exist. Encouraged by this, Mira and her friend searched further, finally discovering clues that led them to the temple's remains.

The journey was thrilling and taught Mira a great deal about history, courage, and perseverance. In the end, she returned home, enriched by the experience, and satisfied with the adventure. Her quest for the lost temple would forever remain one of her most cherished memories.

Author's Profile:

Ishani possesses a profound imagination, emotional sensitivity, and a keen attention to detail. She has a natural talent for crafting intriguing and mysterious narratives that engage and captivate readers. Her ability to connect deeply with human emotions allows her stories to resonate on a personal level.

16

THE JOURNEY TO NATURE WONDERWORLD

– MANVEETA H S

Once upon a time, in a place where the sky was often gray and the rivers were dirty, there lived a young girl named Ria. She loved her home but was sad because it had changed so much. There were not many trees, and the air was hard to breathe. Ria dreamed of a world full of bright colour and clean air.

One day, while walking in a small forest near her house, Ria found a shiny portal hidden behind a big old oak tree. Curious, she stepped through it and discovered a wonderful place called Nature Wonderworld.

In this magical land, the sky was a bright blue, and the air smelled sweet and fresh. Huge flowers bloomed in every colour, and clear rivers flowed happily. Butterflies as big as her hands danced around her, and gentle animals wandered freely. It was a paradise, safe from pollution.

Feeling amazed by the beauty around her, Ria wished with all her heart that her world could be like this. Just then, a wise old turtle came up to her and said, "The magic of

Nature Wonderworld comes from the love and care we give. Share what you've seen with others, and your world can change."

With new hope, Ria went back home, excited to make a difference. She told everyone about her adventure, teaching them to take care of the environment. Little by little, Ria's world began to bloom again, showing the beauty of nature and the power of a dream.

Author's Profile:

Manveetha possesses excellent communication skills that enhance her storytelling and allow her to express ideas with clarity and confidence. Her enthusiasm and proactive nature drive her to seize every opportunity, showcasing her dedication and eagerness to grow. These qualities, combined with her creativity and passion, make her a dynamic and engaging individual, both as a storyteller and as a contributor in any setting.

17

SCARY CREATURE

– NAVNEET P

Strange Creature, it was midnight I was studying. Suddenly I heard a sound in the backyard. At first, I thought there would be no animal. But when I heard it again, I decided to see through the window as it could be any burglar. If it would be then I had to inform the police before he would break into my house.

To my utmost surprise when I saw through the window, I saw a strange creature. At first, I thought it was an animal but when it spoke, I was surprised even more. It was speaking my language. It was telling Help! Help! Help! I could not understand what I would do. I thought" Should I inform my parents." But they were sleeping, and I did not want to disturb them.

I asked him "Who are you and where have you come." He said he was an alien and came from another world. He assured me he would not harm me, but he wanted help from me and requested not to talk about him to anyone. I said" How can I help you?" He said he lost his remote by which he could send a signal to his people. He said to help him to find it as they had a problem seeing without the sun.

I agreed and helped him to find his remote. I found it in the rose bushes. He became incredibly happy and returned home happily.

Author's Profile:

Navneet has natural curiosity about the world, he draws inspiration from everyday life and their experiences, turning them into creative narratives. His passion for storytelling shines through in his ability to think quickly and weave ideas into compelling tales. Always eager to share his work, he demonstrates confidence, creativity, and a love for bringing his stories to life.

18

THE MAGIC IN THE BOTTLE

– AYAANSHI RUNGTA

Once upon a time, there lived a brother and sister. The brother's name was Jack, and the sister's name was Jill. Both Jack and Jill loved chocolates. While coming from school, they saw something glowing under a tree and became curious about it. When they went near the tree, they saw that there was a shiny red bottle and something very small moving inside it.

They wondered what was in that bottle, so they decided to take it home and open it there. When they opened the bottle, a fairy wearing silver glittery clothes appeared. They were still for two minutes. Their house was spined, everything was still.

The fairy Titania took them to Candy Land – the land filled with chocolate. As soon as they entered it rained but, there was no water it rained with gems. There were so many candy canes with white and red stripes. As they walked forward, they found trees covered with 'Choco shots 'as leaves. They jumped to shots and started eating them. They started eating like monsters. Then they realized that there were no clouds but instead, there were 'Dairy milks'.

They climbed onto the dairy milks and reached the top of the candy land. There they could see the mini version of the candy land on a screen. Titania told them to enter the screen and then they would reach their home so, they said Titania bye and left.

MORAL: HAPPINESS IS THE KEY TO PEACE.

Author's Profile:

Ayaanshi is a smart and enthusiastic child with a natural flair for storytelling. Ayanshi's vivid imagination and ability to express emotions through words make her stories captivating, while her enthusiasm infuses her work with energy and charm, leaving a lasting impression on her readers.

19

THE QUEST FOR THE TREASURE CHEST

– PAVITHRA REDDY JAMBULA

Once upon a time, there were four friends—Pavitra, Fathima, Srinika, and Poorvika, who went on a grand adventure with their parents. The parents were on a quest to find something mysterious and scary, and they called the children every day, to update them on the journey. But one day, the parents didn't call.

At first, the children thought their parents were just busy, but later that day, they received a voice message from their mom:

"Travel to the great land of Jungle Bach Challenge Moglie and open the T... Ch!"

And the message was cut off.

The children stared at the screen, confused.

Fathima was the first to speak. "Could it be... Tree Chester?"

The others shook their heads, laughing. "Nooooooo."

"Is it... Tough Chess?" Poorvika asked, her eyes wide with curiosity.

"No," the others replied again.

Pavitra suddenly shouted, "Aaaaaa! Treasure Chest!"

The others gasped. "Ohhhhhh! Might be!"

Excited and determined, the children set off on a journey to find the Treasure Chest. They travelled through deserts, crossed vast seas, and faced many challenges on their way. Finally, after that they felt like an endless journey, they arrived at the land of Jungle Bach.

There, they found Moglie, a powerful figure sitting on his throne. But before they could understand what was happening, something magical occurred. Each of the children received a special power:

- Pavitra got the power of *Jal* (Water),
- Srinika got *Agni* (Fire),
- Fathima received *Vayu* (Wind),
- and Poorvika was given *Prithvi* (Earth).

Together, they used their new powers to defeat Moglie and save the land. When the battle was won, they saw their parents waiting for them with open arms. The children ran to their parents and hugged them tightly, grateful for their help and love.

Everyone thanked the children for their bravery and teamwork. From that day forward, the children knew that no matter how difficult a journey might be, they could always overcome obstacles if they helped others.

And so, they all lived happily ever after.

Moral of the story:

No matter how tough the road is, always help others. You never know what amazing powers and adventures await you!

Author's Profile:

Pavithra's love for reading and her ability to communicate ideas in a structured manner make her a thoughtful and meticulous short story writer. Her reading habit enriches her imagination and provides her with diverse perspectives, which she skillfully incorporates into her narratives. Pavitra creates well-organized plots and cohesive storylines that resonate with readers.

20

THE MAGICAL DOOR TO ADVENTURE

– ANSH JITESH

Amy: "Mom, Dad, can we go out for a break today? Maybe to the park or somewhere fun?"

Mom: "I'm sorry, girls, but your dad and I have a lot of work to get through today. Maybe another time."

Dad: "Yes, we are swamped right now. How about we plan something special for the weekend?"

Lilly: "But we wanted to go out today..."

Amy: "Yeah, we've been cooped up in the house for days!"

Mom: "I understand, sweetie. But sometimes work has to come first. You two can find something fun to do here at home, can't you?"

Lilly: "I guess so..."

Amy: "Hey, here comes Max! Maybe he has some ideas."

Max: "Hi, Lilly! Hi, Amy! What's up?"

Amy: "Our parents are too busy with work to take us out today. We were just thinking of what else we could do."

Max: "Well, I have an idea! Follow me. I found something amazing that I want to show you."

Lilly: "What is it?"

Max: "You'll see. It is a secret. Come on!"

Max leads the sisters to an old door at the back of his garden.

Max: "Here it is. This door is magical. It acts as a teleport to a big island. Want to see?"

Amy: "You're kidding, aren't you?"

Max: "Nope. Just watch."

Max opens the door, and to their amazement, it reveals a path to a lush, green island.

Lilly: "Wow! This is incredible!"

Amy: "Let's go!"

The three friends' step through the door and find themselves on a vast, beautiful island.

Lilly: "This place is amazing. Look at those huge trees!"

Max: "And the flowers! I've never seen anything like them."

Suddenly, a strange creature appears from behind the trees. It is different from anything they have ever seen before, with shimmering scales and glowing eyes.

Creature: "Grrr..."

Amy: "Uh, guys, I think we should run."

Lilly: "Good idea!"

The children start running, with the creature hot on their heels.

Max: "Quick, back to the door!"

They sprint towards the door, hearts pounding, and dive through it just in time.

Amy: "That was close!"

Lilly: "Too close. I think I've had enough adventure for one day."

Max: "Me too. But wasn't it amazing?"

Amy: "Definitely. But maybe next time, let's make sure the place is safe first."

Lilly: "Agreed. Let us go tell Mom and Dad about our adventure!"

The three friends headed back home, excited to share their incredible story.

Author's Profile:

Ansh's pursuit of perfection and strong communication skills make him an exceptional short story writer. His attention to detail ensures his narratives are polished and well-crafted, with no element left to chance. Ansh's clear and effective communication enables him to convey complex ideas and emotions with ease, engaging readers from the start. His dedication to excellence drives him to refine his stories, resulting in narratives that are both captivating and impactful.

SHRIYA PANDEY

AARIN SINGH

ISHANI SALIMATH

NABHAY V

I AM AN AUTHOR

M S DHONI
GLOBAL SCHOOL

KARUNYA K GOWDA

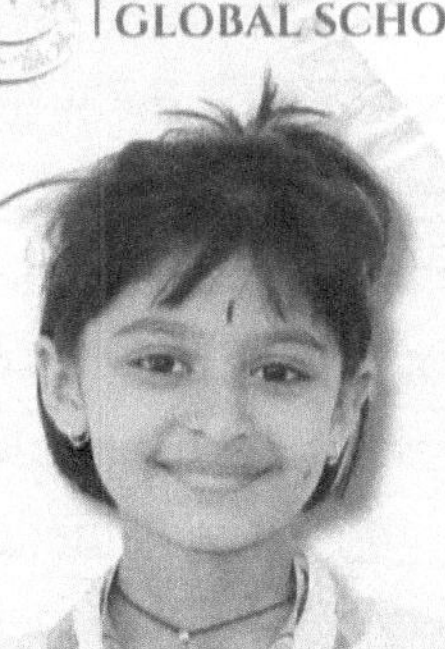

DARSHIK TYAAGI

AADRITI

MANVEETA HS

DHRUTI P

AYAANSHI RUNGTA

21

THE TALENTED THIEF

– SAANVI BALIYAR SINGH

Claudia lived in a magical city with her friends, Amy, Li, Maya, Zoie, and Scarlett, who were from another planet. A talented thief took and trapped the people who made their dreams come true. The talent thief lived on the same planet as Claudia and her friends; he came to Earth to steal the talent.

After some time, the girls found out that the talent thief is trapping all the people who make their dreams come true in 'DREAMLAND!' Claudia said, 'Whatever we do, we have to be quick because we cannot let all the people get trapped forever!' she told panicking, Zoie said ' I have put a GPS tracker on his back……. And he is in France!' 'Let's go there then.' Said Li. They finally reached France; it took them 17 hours to get there in an aeroplane from Las Vegas. They found the 'Institute François de la Mode!' which is a fashion academy, and they were sure that the talent thief was there because there were a lot of people who had a talent in fashion like modelling, designing, etc…….but the talent thief is good in hiding, he can even camouflage! Maya said, 'Keep your eyes and ears open because his magic is stronger than ours.' 'True….' said Amy.

After some time, they found the talented thief and started chasing him, but he escaped through a portal to dreamland, and the girls decided to teleport him there. They went there and got into a maze with trees, 'Dear tree, can you please show us the exit.' chanted Li, and then the trees led the path, and they got out, then they defeated the talent thief together, but still he was able to escape. 'We used direct magic on him now let's use indirect magic.' said Zoie, and it worked! They had defeated him. Then they rescued the people and returned home. 'We will go to Earth and help people when they are in danger.' promised the girls.

MORAL: Always help others when they are in need.

Author's Profile:

Saanvi has good command of language, and this helps her to convey emotions and ideas with clarity and flair. Saanvi's ability to communicate effectively allows her to connect with readers, drawing them into her stories. Her creativity and attention to detail ensure her narratives are both captivating and thought-provoking, making her a promising short story writer.

22

SMOKEY'S CHRISTMAS GIFT

– CRAIG MITCHELL N

Smokey the Cat is looking out of his window. He is very grumpy. His mother has refused to get the latest toy mouse in the Jingle Bells series. Also, she told him to give away some of his toys!

"Mother" called Smokey. "Why aren't you getting me that mouse?"

"Smokey, I have told you many times that I and your father are getting you a surprise. Also, you must give some of your toys to sick children at the hospital."

"Why?" asked Smokey. "Christmas is about getting gifts, right?"

"No, Smokey. Christmas is about showing the love of Jesus to everyone. Also, you are becoming very naughty and rude. It would do you good not to have your way for once!" said Mother.

"But Mother, Mittens has one, so does Socks and Tiger too!" whined Smokey. "And so does…"

"No more whining." said his mother firmly. "Straight to bed!"

"But…," said Smokey.

"I said BED!" shouted his mother, reaching for the rolling pin. Smokey ran to his room. It fell asleep at once. Suddenly, he saw a bright light falling from the sky. One of them landed next to Smokey. It was a cat! And not just any cat it looked like his friend Whiskers!

"Whiskers?" asked Smokey. "What happened to you?"

"I turned into an angel!" smiled Whiskers.

Smokey looked at the other lights. "Are the Angels too?" he asked.

"Yes." Replied Whiskers. "Now, come to my horse. We must go on a journey."

"Yeh!' said Smokey, "A journey!" and they got on the horse and rode towards a hospital.

"Is that Caring Paws Hospital?" Smokey asked Whiskers. "My mother wanted me to give my toys here!"

Whiskers and Smokey went to the hospital. They entered a room. A little kitten, about four months old, was sobbing in a bed.

"Oh No!" whispered Smokey. "What happened to him?"

"He has a contagious disease", answered Whiskers seriously.

"No one can visit him, so he is lonely. He won't get anything for Christmas, and there are no toys to play with."

"Look! You are so blessed! Yet, you cannot give away a few old toys?"

"Oh! Whiskers, I am so sorry! cried Smokey. "I will give my toys tomorrow."

"Good" smiled Whisker. "Goodbye! My job is done, Smokey."

"Smokey! Wake up!" Smokey woke up to find his mother shaking him.

"Mummy, I want to go and give my toys to Caring Paws Hospital." His mother looked shocked.

She then smiled and said, "Good boy, Smokey" and hugged him.

Author's Profile:

Craig's natural leadership qualities and proactive nature make him a dynamic short story writer. His ability to take initiative allows him to explore bold ideas and tackle challenging themes with confidence. Craig's enthusiasm and drive ensure he pours energy and creativity into his narratives, crafting stories that inspire and engage his audience.

23

THE MAGICAL WORLD INSIDE THE DOOR

– DARSHIK TYAAGI

Mag was a boy who believed in magic. He loved pretending to be a magician and admired superheroes on TV. One night, he discovered a door he had never noticed before. As he opened it, he found himself in an amazing, magical world—colors filled the sky, and butterflies danced around him, leading him down a glowing path.

With each step, amazing things happened. On the ninth step, colorful lights lit up; on the tenth, tiny glowing insects appeared. On the final step, fantastic creatures welcomed him with cheers and a shower of candies and chocolates.

The king of this magical world greeted Mag, saying, "You're invited to join us for one day!" Mag quickly learned he had magical powers here. When he clapped, water appeared; when he snapped, food arrived; and objects he touched came alive. Lunch was a feast around a huge bonfire, with candies, chocolates, and burgers, and Mag played games with his new friends—cricket, ludo, and more.

After a nap, they joined hands and chanted a magical mantra that filled the air with warmth and energy. Dinner was just as delightful, and they laughed and shared stories under the shimmering sky.

As the day ended, the king told Mag, "You are always welcome. Believe in magic, and the door will open again." Mag waved goodbye to his friends, stepping back into his world, and the door disappeared behind him.

From that night on, Mag never stopped believing in magic, knowing that the world held endless wonders just waiting to be found.

Author's Profile:

With a natural talent for weaving thrilling adventures and creating captivating characters, Darshik demonstrates a strong sense of empathy and an understanding of human emotions. Darshik's passion for mythical storytelling reveals his curiosity and dedication, while his vivid descriptions showcase his knack for painting pictures with words. These qualities make him a visionary writer capable of transporting readers to extraordinary realms.

24

THE GREAT ESCAPE

– SPANDANA R V

A puppy opened its eyes to the world. It has been a few weeks since it was brought to the world. Along it lay its four other siblings, His mother started slowly and calmly saying the pup's names out loud. "Mooncake, Sunshine, Skylight, and Ari."

Ari was a chocolate brown dog with a nice, warm smiley face and a soft, bushy tail.

Mooncake was a white fluffy puppy.

Sunshine was a bright, golden-brown puppy with a swirly tail.

Skylight was a mix of brown and white, with a black base and a beautiful curly tail.

They were born on a beach in Mumbai. It was a sunny morning, and it had just started drizzling. The mother was soon exhausted by hunting food for herself and feeding the puppies. She soon fell asleep under the shade of a small plant. The pups were also tired and a bit sleepy. There was no space under the plant, and it was about to rain. The pups began to wander in search of a place to sleep.

They saw a huge van pull up. Out came a big man with a bushy beard and a small guy, who was about twenty years old. The big man had a hideous grin on his face. He turned to the little man and chuckled, "Ay, get the nets! We got bounty o'er here!" Soon, it turned all dark for the pups. They could not see anything.

After what seemed like days, the puppies woke up, and to their surprise, they were locked up in a cage. Ari and Sunshine were in a cage, and Mooncake and Skylight were in another cage.

They looked around and saw many other little puppies like themselves.

"What have we done!" said Sunlight. "We should have never wandered off in the rain! I want to go back to our mother! I mean… *I* am not scared, but mother might be. I am not scared at all!" she said, trembling.

Ari reassured Sunlight, "Do not worry, we will find a way out of this place." Skylight and Mooncake were in the cage opposite Ari and Sunlight. They discussed their plans to try to escape. They could see a door outside. It was more like a large, open window with vertical railings. They could see the streets of Mumbai and faraway, they could see the beach.

After some time, they noticed the little man pop a new pup inside a cage. They carefully saw the way he opened the crate. Now, the pups knew how to open the cage from the OUTSIDE, but not from the inside. They tried licking the latch open, and banging the door with their paws and nothing worked. Finally, Mooncake bit the edge of the latch and slightly tugged it, and finally, the door was open. Now, all they had to do was push the door to the crate and escape through the door.

Suddenly, the big man appeared and checked on all the dogs. He said "Do not worry, you little puppies! I will soon find you a buyer…" and he let out an evil laugh "Mwuhahahaha!!!!" he giggled. He left after some time.

"Whew!" said Sunshine. "That was close…" They waited for a few minutes, just in case the big man decided to swing by and do a quick check (again).

Finally, Skylight pushed the door open and opened the door to Ari and Sunshine's cage.

They were just about to slip through the railings of the big door, when they heard a voice say, "STOP!" Skylight turned around, just to see the other pups waiting. "Aren't you going to free us too?"

The four pups looked at each other and nodded. They quietly opened the cage and freed the other pups. "I've been waiting for months!" One of them said.

The pups quickly slipped through the railings of the big door and ran as fast as they could.

The four pups made it to the beach, but they could not find the mother.

They trembled in fear… What might have happened? Did she wander off and get lost? Or worse; did she get caught by the big man? IS SHE DEAD!?

While the pups were wondering, their mother crept back on them, and said (angrily) "Where have you pups been? I have been looking for you all over the beach! Could you not tell me if you were leaving at least?...." and she continued.

The pups looked at each other and had a sense of relief from finding their "lost" mom, but only for a second. They were given a long lecture on not going anywhere and staying close to the mother no matter what and so on…

Author's Profile:

Spandana expresses her thoughts with clarity and confidence. Her writing skills are outstanding, showcasing creativity and depth well beyond her years. She is admired for her way with words, often looking forward to her insightful essays and stories. Her talent shines brightly in every piece she writes, making her a standout in both her written and verbal expressions.

25

THE MYSTERY OF THE MIDNIGHT DREAM

– K SAHANA

It was a dark, stormy night when Jason felt something was wrong. The wind howled through the empty streets, and the rain lashed against the ground, like tiny needles. His shoes stopped on the wet pavement as he walked home from his best friend's house. The city felt unusually quiet—too quiet for such a rainy night. Jason pulled his jacket tighter around his shoulders and glanced over his shoulder. No one. But… it still felt like someone was following him.

His heart began to race as a flash of lightning split the sky, lighting up the entire street. For that split second, Jason saw it—a shadowy figure standing at the far end of the road. The figure was tall, maybe even taller than any person Jason knew, and it stood, like it was waiting for him.

Thunder rumbled, low and deep, shaking the ground beneath him. He quickened his pace, trying to convince himself it was just the storm playing tricks on his mind. But with every step, he felt the presence behind him. The footstep seemed to follow his own. Jason dared a glance behind him, but saw nothing. The street was empty. Still, he couldn't shake the feeling that something was off.

Another flash of lightning, brighter this time, lit up the street again. And in the flicker of light, the figure was closer. Much closer.

Jason's heart pounded in his chest, and fear gripped him. He turned and broke into a full sprint, the rain now pouring down harder than ever. The wind whipped his face, and the thunder seemed to follow him, crashing so loudly it felt like the whole world was about to break apart. Yet no matter how fast he ran, the footsteps kept pace. He looked over his shoulder again—there was no figure, but he could hear it. The unmistakable sound of someone—or something—right behind him.

Suddenly, his foot caught on something in the dark. He tripped, falling to the ground with a sickening thud. His head spun as he scrambled to his feet. But when he looked up, the world had changed. The street, once familiar, was now unrecognizable. The rain had stopped, and the sky above was swirling with strange, unnatural colours—purple, green, and gold. The air crackled with an unreal energy, as though the storm had broken the laws of nature itself.

Jason stumbled forward, trying to make sense of what was happening. He turned around, desperate to find something—anything—to explain the bizarre scene. The figure was gone, but he could still feel its presence. It was like it was everywhere watching him, waiting for him.

The wind howled louder than ever, and Jason's heart raced in his chest. He didn't know where to go or what to do. He felt completely alone in this strange, twisted world. And then, as if out of nowhere, a voice broke through the chaos.

"Jason… Jason, wake up."

It was his mother's voice. Soft, familiar, and warm.

Jason blinked. The swirling colours in the sky faded, and the strange energy vanished. His legs were no longer shaky, and his heart was no longer pounding. Slowly, his surroundings began to return to normal. He was lying in his own bed, the soft glow of his nightlight casting a gentle shadow on the walls. The storm had passed, and everything was calm.

"Mom?" Jason mumbled, rubbing his eyes as he tried to wake up.

His mother was standing in the doorway of his room, her face filled with concern. "You were having a nightmare, Jason. You were calling out in your sleep."

Jason's heart slowly returned to a normal rhythm. It had all been a dream. Just a dream.

He sat up in bed, still trying to shake off the strange feeling that lingered in his chest. But as he looked out the window at the clear night sky, he couldn't help but wonder if there had been something more to it. The storm, the figure, the strange colors—none of it made sense.

Was it just his imagination running wild? Or was there something more—something he hadn't fully understood?

"Are you okay?" his mom asked, walking over to sit beside him on the bed.

Jason nodded, but his mind was still numb. He couldn't shake the feeling that the dream was trying to tell him something, something important. But for now, he pushed the thoughts aside. He was safe, warm, and back in his world.

Author's Profile:

Sahana, is a dedicated and sincere student. Her written work reflects a deep commitment to learning, with every line crafted thoughtfully and precisely. Beyond academics, she shines brightly in dance, her movements graceful and expressive, capturing the essence of every beat. Her love for music is equally profound, as her voice carries both strength and emotion. In all she does, she exemplifies passion, discipline, and a natural elegance that inspires everyone around her.

26

THE WHISPERING GROVE

– RIYANSHI MAHESHWARI

Deep in the heart of Valora Forest lay the Whispering Grove, a mystical place where the trees, thousands of years old, shared their secrets with those who would listen. Naya, a curious and adventurous young elf, had always longed to visit the Grove. Her grandmother often told her stories of how the trees imparted wisdom to the brave souls who sought them out. One crisp autumn morning, with leaves dancing in the wind, Naya decided it was time.

Naya ventured deep into the woods, her steps light and heart full of hope. As she approached the Grove, she heard the gentle murmurs of the ancient oaks and maples. Kneeling on the mossy ground, Naya closed her eyes and listened intently. "Seek balance," whispered an oak. "Trust in patience," murmured a maple. Their words swirled around her, soothing and gentle. Yet, just as she began to feel content, a birch tree sighed, "Beware the lure of rushing. "Curious, Naya opened her eyes to see a bright, golden light shimmering ahead. Drawn to its beauty, she felt a pull to hurry forward. But remembering the birch's warning, she stopped, breathing deeply and slowing her thoughts.

Gradually, the light faded, and in its place appeared a path of shimmering emerald leaves. Naya smiled, understanding Grove's lesson. She made her way home, feeling wiser and more in tune with the forest's rhythm.

Moral: Wisdom often lies in patience and balance, even when life tempts you to rush ahead.

Author's Profile:

Riyanshi has a flair for writing and a heart full of compassion. Her stories often reflect her gentle nature, weaving in themes of kindness and empathy. Her peers admire her for her sensitivity and understanding, and she's a trusted friend who listens with genuine care. Riyanshi dreams of using her writing to make a positive impact on the world around her.

27

THE MILK MAN

– ADITYA HEGDE

CHAPTER 1 (A Monster is Born)

Once upon a time, there was a milkman named Henry. He wakes up at four in the morning, milks his cow, and gets ready to deliver the milk around five am. One day he had to deliver milk to an old mansion that had been abandoned for around two years now. He took his milk bottles and went to the mansion. When he arrived, he rang the doorbell" DING DONG DING DONG" the doorbell rang. The door opened by itself with a s mall creaking sound. He went in expecting someone inside. When he stepped inside, the door shut all by itself with a loud bang! Henry gasped with fright, it was very dark inside, but all of a sudden, the lights turned on. He saw a small pedestal; on the pedestal it was written: keep milk bottle on top of the pedestal".As the writing said, Henry kept the milk bottle on top of the pedestal. Suddenly the bottle of milk turned into a bottle of blood! All of a sudden the lights switched off. Henry couldn't see anything. All of a sudden he saw a glowing light behind a door. Henry was hesitant at first but then he tried to open the door but it turned out to be locked from the inside. He tried to open the door a second time and it opened. There was a floating orb that was producing all that light. After he saw the orb he felt weird, as if he was attracted to it. All of a sudden he went and touched it, then after he touched it he got teleported back to his house! He felt very creeped out and weird so he went and took a rest.

In the evening he got up and decided to go for a small walk. But when he noticed that his skin colour was black! his eyes were white! Now Henry was more than human, he was now something else.

CHAPTER 2 (The Mansion)

Henry thought of going to the mansion again and thinking that touching the orb again would cure him, but little did he know it was going to get worse. When he entered the mansion again he sensed something had changed. He could now see in the dark! Henry was shocked to discover such a possibility in him. Now that he could see in the dark he wanted to explore the mansion in detail to see what he could find in the other story of the mansion. On the second floor, Henry found a room which was locked, he started to look for the key because that was the only room on that floor. Henry then went to the first floor and found a hidden door with a

swimming pool inside, but it was no ordinary swimming pool. The pool was filled with blood! Then Henry heard footsteps coming from the room where he found the orb. Then after a blink something jumped scared him, forcing him to jump into the pool of blood! Then the footsteps had disappeared without a trace. Henry peaked out a bit to see if anyone was there, no one but a small key lying on the floor. Henry quickly got out of the pool to take the key when suddenly all the blood drained from the pool all on its own!

CHAPTER 3 (A New Friend)

Henry quickly went upstairs and checked I the key fit the lock of the locked room it did not He thought it was for a closet or a safe or another door, but he did not care much about it so he put the key in his pocket and moved on exploring the rest of the mansion. He soon found a room in the corner of the mansion which had a light on. He opened the door and found a guy sitting on a chair. He spoke with a soft voice" Hello there Henry "

Henry replied, "How do you know my name?". Then the man spoke, "I know everything about you".The man later introduced himself as Jack and he wanted to help Henry. Then Jack vanished into thin air and dropped another key. Then Henry called out to Jack, and he appeared. Henry showed him the key that he had found earlier in the pool room. Jack said that it was a key for a brewing room which was inside the locked room upstairs. Then again Jack disappeared into thin air.

CHAPTER 4 (A DREAM)

Henry immediately ran to the room on the second floor and unlocked it. The room looked like a normal bedroom, but Henry took a closer look, and he found a hidden door hidden in the wall, he tried the key which he found in the pool room, and it opened. He found the brewing room just like Jack said. Luckey for him still used to remember some chemistry lessons from when he was in high school times. Then after a lot of long and messy tries he had it, a cure. All of a sudden Jack appeared and said" We have enjoyed our time with you" and just vanished. Henry drank the cure and he was a bit disappointed in the taste, but nothing was happening. All of a sudden Henry felt very tired and fainted. He woke up in his hut all normal and realized all of this was just a dream." Or was it?"

Author's Profile:

Aditya is a cheerful young boy who lights up every room with his infectious enthusiasm and warm smile. He brings joy to all he does, whether it's academics, sports, or helping classmates, making every activity enjoyable for himself and those around him. He holds deep respect for elders, always greeting them with politeness and listening attentively to their advice. His kindness and respectful nature make him a favourite among teachers and peers alike. With his positive attitude, he is an inspiration to everyone he meets.

28

THE SECRET OF THE BLACK COIN

– MRIDHIMA AGARWAL

Mira Graves is a smart and determined young detective working on a high-profile case—the mysterious death of a famous businessman, Victor Haines. At first, it seems like just another case, but as the investigation unfolds, Mira discovers a trail of strange clues that lead her to a much darker secret—one that could change everything she thought she knew about the people around her.

Mira stumbles upon a strange coin with a mysterious symbol. At first, she thinks it's a coincidence, but after finding several more of these coins, she realizes they might be part of a much bigger story. Each coin seems to point to a different location that she and her best friend, Ethan, used to visit as kids. She connects the dots: these places hold a deeper significance, and she begins to suspect that her investigation is leading her closer to something far more dangerous than a simple murder.

Mira trusts Ethan completely—he's her childhood friend and confidant. She tells him everything about her investigation. He listens patiently, offers advice, and encourages her to keep going. But as Mira investigates further, she notices small, odd things about Ethan—things that don't quite add up.

Mira realizes that Ethan is somehow connected to the very conspiracy she's investigating, but she refuses to believe it. She doesn't want to consider the possibility that the one person she's trusted the most could be hiding something so dark.

Mira goes to Ethan's house to confront him, feeling that something is wrong. When she arrives, she sneaks inside and follows a trail of clues that leads her to a hidden basement. There, she discovers a room with a collection of strange items and documents tied to powerful figures in the city—people who have been secretly controlling events from the shadows.

Ethan appears and reveals that he's been involved with a secret organization—The Black Circle, a group that wields influence over business and politics in the city. He tells her that the investigation has gone too far, and she now knows too much.

Mira is shocked and heartbroken by the betrayal. She confronts Ethan, demanding answers. He admits that he's been involved in shady dealings but insists that he never wanted to hurt her. He tells her that now that she knows the truth, she'll be in danger if she tries to expose it.

Tensions rise as Mira struggles to reconcile the friend; she thought she knew the person standing before her now. She knows that she can't ignore what she's discovered, but at the same time, she feels conflicted about turning her back on someone she's trusted for so long.

With Ethan threatening to stop her from going public, Mira must make a choice. She manages to escape the confrontation and races to tell her superior, Captain Lyle, everything she's uncovered. The captain is shocked but agrees to help her expose the truth.

However, as Mira begins to gather evidence, the group behind the conspiracy makes one final attempt to stop her. She is faced with the challenge of outsmarting them and bringing the truth to light without putting herself or others in danger.

Mira decides to confront Ethan one last time. They have a final, tense conversation where Ethan admits his wrongdoings but expresses regret for dragging Mira into this world. He offers her a choice: to leave everything behind and forget what she's learned or to fight for justice and expose the truth to the world. Mira must decide whether to forgive her old friend or stop him once and for all.

Mira stands at the threshold of the hidden room in Ethan's mansion, staring at the man who has been her best friend for years. The shock of everything she's uncovered still courses through her veins. The strange coins, the shady meetings, the connections to powerful people—it all makes sense now. And yet, the person she thought she knew, the one she trusted with her life, was someone completely different.

Ethan looks at her with regret in his eyes, but there's also an air of resignation as if he knows this moment has been coming for a long time.

Ethan: "I never wanted you to get involved, Mira. I wanted to protect you from all of this. But you're too smart—you always were. I knew it was only a matter of time before you figured it out. I didn't want to hurt you, but I've made choices. And those choices have consequences."

Mira's heart is torn. She's spent her whole life relying on Ethan. Their friendship was something she always believed to be unbreakable. But now, as she looks at him, she sees the truth: the world he's been living in is darker and more dangerous than anything she could have imagined. And yet, a part of her wants to believe that this isn't the Ethan she grew up with—the one who would never hurt anyone, the one who would help her solve any case, no matter how difficult.

Mira: "Why, Ethan? Why didn't you tell me? We could have figured something out together. I trusted you, and now... I don't even know who you are anymore."

Ethan takes a step toward her, his expression conflicted. "I didn't want to pull you into this world. I thought I could keep you safe. But now, you know too much. And there's no turning back."

Mira's thoughts race. She's spent days following the trail, connecting all the clues, only to realize that the most dangerous one was the person closest to her. She feels the weight of the decision before her: does she protect Ethan, the friend she's known her entire life, or does she bring everything to light, no matter the cost?

Mira knows there's no easy way out. She's already uncovered too much. If she walks away now, the truth could be buried forever, and more people could get hurt. But if she exposes Ethan, she risks losing everything—her friendship, her trust in herself, and even her future.

But Mira is a detective. She's always believed that the truth, no matter how painful, is the most important thing. She looks at Ethan one last time, her heart heavy with the weight of what she's about to do.

Mira: "I can't let you get away with this, Ethan. I won't be part of your secret anymore. You've made your choices, but I can't be the one to protect you from the consequences. I have to stop this."

Ethan's face falls, his eyes showing a flicker of the old friend she once knew, but then his resolve hardens.

Ethan: "If you go through with this, Mira, you'll never be safe. Do you think you can walk away from me? You think I won't find you? You're making a huge mistake."

Mira: "Maybe. But I'd rather make a mistake standing up for what's right than live with the guilt of letting this continue. I don't care what it costs. The truth matters."

With those final words, Mira turns and runs out of the room, her mind set on what she must do. She knows she's not just running away from Ethan, but from everything she thought she knew. But she also knows that in doing so, she's stepping into the light, even if it means facing the unknown.

Mira races to the police headquarters, her heart pounding in her chest. She's not sure what will happen when she tells Captain Lyle everything—when she exposes Ethan and the dangerous syndicate, he's been a part of. But she knows it's the only way.

When she bursts into her boss's office, she tells him everything: about the Black Circle, the corruption, the secrets Ethan has been hiding, and how deep this conspiracy runs. The captain listens, his expression grave, but he knows this is bigger than they ever imagined. He promises to take the necessary steps to expose the truth.

Days pass. The investigation into the Black Circle intensifies, and soon enough, the organization is exposed to the world. People are arrested, and the powerful figures behind the syndicate are brought to justice. But for Mira, the victory feels bittersweet. The case is solved, but the price of the truth is high.

Ethan disappears after exposure, his fate unknown. Mira doesn't know if she'll ever see him again—or if she should. She's learned the hard way that some bonds, no matter how strong, can't survive when lies and secrets tear them up.

A Few Years Later...

Mira Graves sat in her office at the precinct, working through a pile of case files. The noise of the busy office faded into the background as she lost herself in the work. It had been years since the collapse of the Black Circle, and Mira had come a long way since then. She had solved many cases, earned the trust of her colleagues, and built a solid reputation as one of the most dedicated detectives on the force.

But despite all her professional success, there were still days when she couldn't shake the memories of Ethan—the friend she had once trusted with everything, the betrayal that had shattered her trust, and the painful realization that he had been living a double life.

The door creaked open, and Mira glanced up, expecting a new case file or a colleague with a question. But what she saw made her freeze.

Standing in the doorway was Ethan—the man who had once been her best friend, the person who had hurt her the most.

His appearance had changed over the years. He wore a well-tailored suit, his hair was neatly styled, and his posture was confident, but there was something softer about him now—something genuine. Gone was the shadow of the man who had been involved with the dangerous Black Circle. In his place stood a man who seemed determined to make amends.

For a long moment, Mira didn't know how to react.

Mira: "Ethan…"

His name felt strange on her tongue, like a word she hadn't said in years.

Ethan stepped into the room, his expression calm, but there was a glimmer of hope in his eyes.

Ethan: "It's r you, Mira. I didn't know if you'd want to see me, but I had to try. After all this time, I owe you an explanation. And more than that—I owe you the truth."

Mira stood up, her heart pounding in her chest. She hadn't expected to see him again, especially not like this. The betrayal still stung, but she could also see the sincerity in his eyes. He wasn't the same person who had walked out of her life all those years ago.

Mira: "I don't know if I'm ready for this, Ethan. You hurt me. You betrayed my trust in the worst possible way."

Ethan nodded; his expression filled with regret.

Ethan: "I know. And I don't expect forgiveness right away. I've had time to reflect on everything I did—and everything I lost because of it. I understand if you hate me. But I've spent these years trying to make things right. I left that life behind. I built a new life—one that doesn't involve lies or betrayal."

Mira studied him for a long time. She remembered the old Ethan—the one who had been there for her through thick and thin, the one who had always made her laugh, the one she had trusted more than anyone else in the world. She wanted to believe him. But after everything that had happened, she wasn't sure how to move forward.

Mira: "So what do you want from me? Why come to me now?"

Ethan: "I don't expect anything from you. I just want you to know that I've changed. I've worked hard to make amends. And I've come to ask if maybe... if maybe we could start over."

There was a long pause. Mira felt the weight of his words, the quiet sincerity in his voice. She had spent years trying to move past the pain of their betrayal, and yet here he was, offering her a chance to rebuild. But the road to forgiveness wasn't easy, and the scars of the past were not so easily erased.

Mira: "I don't know, Ethan. You hurt me. You hurt a lot of people. I've learned to trust other people, to trust myself again. I don't know if I can just... pick up where we left off."

Ethan's face fell, but there was no bitterness in his expression— only understanding.

Ethan: "I don't expect you to forget. I don't expect you to forgive me right away. But I'm asking for the chance to prove that I'm not the person I was. That I can be the friend you once knew—and more than that, someone who can be worthy of your trust again."

Mira's heart felt heavy. It was difficult to hear those words, and even harder to know if she was ready to believe them. But deep down, she couldn't deny that there was still a part of her that wanted to believe in the Ethan she once knew.

She took a deep breath, searching for the right words.

Mira: "I don't know how this is going to work. But... maybe we can try. Maybe we can start over—slowly. But it's going to take time. And trust, once it's broken, doesn't come back overnight."

Ethan's eyes softened, and for the first time in years, Mira saw the old spark of hope in them.

Ethan: "I'll wait as long as it takes. I'll prove it to you, Mira. One day at a time."

Over the next few months, Mira and Ethan took small steps toward rebuilding their friendship. It wasn't easy. There were awkward silences, moments where Mira had to remind herself to trust him, and times when Ethan had to show that he had truly changed. But slowly, piece by piece, they began to find their way back to each other.

Ethan had kept his promise. He had left the underworld behind and had worked hard to build a legitimate business, focusing on helping communities and giving back in ways he had never done before. He even partnered with several charities that Mira had supported in the past, showing that he wasn't just talking about change—he was living it.

Mira watched him grow, not just as a businessman, but as a person. The more she saw him work to make things right, the more she began to believe in his transformation.

One evening, as they sat at a quiet café, just like they had when they were younger, Mira looked across the table at Ethan. His smile was the same as it had been years ago— warm, easy, and genuine.

Mira: "You've changed, haven't you?"

Ethan's smile softened, and he nodded.

Ethan: "Yeah. I had to. For myself. For you. And for everyone I let down."

Mira smiled back, the tension between them easing, though there was still a part of her that would never forget what had happened. But as they sat there, she realized that she had come to trust him again, not because of the past, but because of the person he was now.

Mira: "I'm glad you're back, Ethan. I don't know what the future holds, but... it feels good to have you back in my life."

Ethan reached across the table, his hand resting gently on hers. It wasn't an overtly romantic gesture, but one that spoke of the bond they were slowly rebuilding—of the friendship that was stronger for having weathered such a storm.

Ethan: "I won't let you down again, Mira. I promise."

As they sat there together, for the first time in years, Mira felt the weight of the past lift off her shoulders. They weren't the same people they had been before—but maybe, just maybe, they were something even better. Two people who had learned from their mistakes and were ready to start again, stronger than before.

Mira and Ethan had both changed. The road to redemption wasn't easy, and their friendship had been tested in ways neither of them had ever imagined. But through time, patience, and a willingness to rebuild from the ashes of the past, they found their way back to each other.

They knew there would be challenges ahead, but for now, they were content in knowing that, no matter what had happened before, they had been given the chance to start again.

And this time, they would do it right.

Author's Profile:

Mridhima is a bright and diligent girl who combines her love for writing with a deep commitment to her studies. Known for her attention to detail, she tackles every assignment with precision and care, always striving for excellence. Her compassionate nature makes her a friend to all, as she's quick to help classmates and offer words of encouragement.

29

THE GRAVEYARD

– AMONA CHAVADI

Soundlessly, I walked through the rugged pathway. The fluorescent moon illuminated the deserted cemetery, and the overcast sky was enveloped with angry clouds. Despite this, I could see the freckles of silver stars hanging from the sky.

The first thing I noticed was the damp grass beneath me which was covered with fallen, crumpled leaves. When my eyes adjusted to the darkness, I took a look at the surroundings, covered with towering trees and an iron gate that had steadily opened due to the gust of wind. When I attempted to get up, I felt a thug on my head. I leaned against a spine tree to regain my vision. With a minute's rest, I tried to walk forward unbalanced, weak, cold. I twisted my hands to examine them. Once deathly pale they were now almost blue. Goosebumps and shivers raced up my arms and my thoughts ran by. Walking a few more steps, I got trapped in an unusual, closed forest. Squinching my eyes, I noticed withered, dried flowers falling on the ground, and weird blood stains scattered over mud.

The moment when I realized, after the view of several graves, that I was stuck in an eerie graveyard. Just then, I heard the thumping of footsteps coming from a certain distance. A gush of cold wind suddenly comes by and I realize I shouldn't be here any longer. Trying my best, with my limping leg, I ran as fast as I could, panting as loud as a lion. Hearing the sound of the footsteps coming closer, my heart starts racing and beating as fast as it ever can. When I had to stop to catch my breath, I realized what was after I was lost. But just then I saw an open grave in front of me and a sudden eerie silence. As I turned back, I saw a sight that made me sigh with big regret for what I said earlier. Well, it was too late…

Author's Profile:

Amona is a curious and passionate individual with a love for exploring new ideas and asking thought-provoking questions. With an adventurous spirit and a fearless attitude, she thrives on challenges and brings an innovative perspective to her writing. Her vivid imagination and ability to weave engaging narratives reflect her dynamic personality, making her stories both impactful and memorable.

30

THE SCENT OF SUSPICION

– SHRIYA PANDEY

In a city haunted by darkness, a series of murders unfolds in a renowned museum. Each victim is posed, frozen in sickening yet beautiful imitation of the sculptures around them, a vision crafted by a sinister artist with a twisted sense of beauty. The murderer, known as "the Artist," leaves only one calling card at each crime scene—a mysterious, haunting scent of perfume lingering in the air, a clue as delicate yet ominous as the silence that fills the museum's marble halls. Leo, a prodigious detective, is assigned to the case along with his team—Astrea, Ace, and Aria.

Known for his exceptional intellect and skill, Leo has solved some of the most impenetrable mysteries, earning him both admiration and resentment. Astrea, his rival, despises him deeply; though her brilliance matches his own, his genius has cast a long shadow over her efforts. But this case would demand the best from them all and would push their fragile trust to its breaking point. The very interpretation of Leo's name was a constellation with bright stars. Astrea's name served an important role as well, her name denoted the goddess of justice Even the detective who was considered a prodigy seemed baffled at this unique case.

As the case carried on, Leo's off behavior wasn't left unnoticed, especially by Ace and Astrea. Leo constantly grumbled that the museum only contained meaningless art and that true art didn't get adequate opportunity to prove itself. He complained how in auctions the bidders spend their fortune away on art that appears as if it were made by a toddler.

Author's Profile:

Shriya is passionate about writing and has a curious mind that never rests. She spends hours crafting stories, letting her imagination soar with each word she pens. Always eager to explore the world around her, Shriya draws inspiration from nature, people, and even the smallest details in everyday life. Her writings brim with creativity and reflect her deep understanding of emotions and experiences. With dreams of becoming an author, she's constantly exploring new ideas, pushing her creative boundaries every day.

CHAKRAVARTHY SASSIKUMAR

PAVITHRA REDDY JAMBULA

NAINIKA KANIKE

SAANVI BALIYAR SINGH

I AM AN AUTHOR

 M S DHONI GLOBAL SCHOOL

KYRA BAGGA

CHIRAG VASANTH

CRAIG MITCHELL N

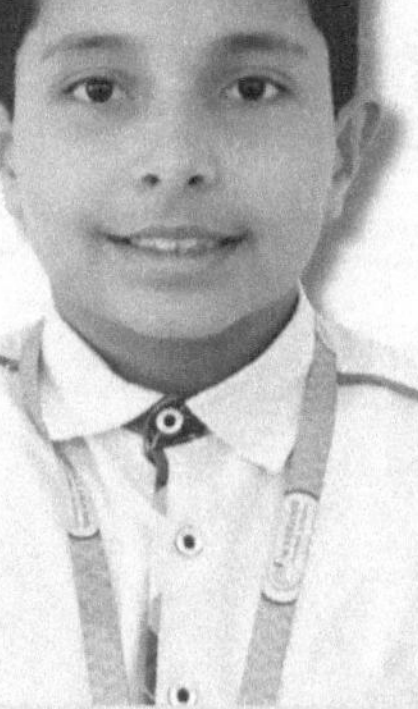

NAVANEETH P

ANSH JITESH

SRIRANJINI K